I0731774

Alarico

hidden journals volume 2

Elle Klass

*Award winning author
of mystery and suspense*

Alarico hidden journals volume 2

Copyright © 2020 by Books by
Elle, Inc.
225 College Dr. #65504
Orange Park Fl, 32065
ISBN: 978-1-951017-14-9
Cover art created by TL Katt
Editor Dawn Lewis Bookmarks
Editing
Website: elleklass.weebly.com

Author's Disclaimer

Other books by Elle

The Bloodseekers: St. Augustine Novellas
The Vampires Next Door Book 1
The Monster Upstairs Book 2
The Ghost Within Book 3

hidden journals
Isandro
Alarico

Zombie Girl
Premonition Book 1
Infection Book 2
Retribution Book 3

Baby Girl
In the Beginning Volume 1
Moonlighting in Paris Volume 2
City by the Bay Volume 3
Bite the Big Apple Volume 4
Caribbean Heat Volume 5
Return to the Bay Volume 6
Prison of the Past Volume 7
Baby Girl Box Set - Volumes 1-4

Alarico hidden journals volume 2

preface

The world peaceful and the magic balanced, the Slayers moved on with their lives. They finished high school, went to college, and started careers. By thirty they realized they weren't aging. People were beginning to notice. It was time to leave their present lives. Mandy and the wolves went to Wolf Manor and she started an ecommerce store selling herbal remedies that she spelled with healing magic. Vicky traveled the world working as a freelance photographer and journalist. Opal and Rylan settled in his home country of Spain, in the mountains, where she took an interest in antiques. Lacey worked her way up in the fashion design world, started her own line, and designed on the move. Adrian wrote code and designed video games from home. Rodham and Alison started an online bookstore. It was her idea. The plan was to have a child when the business got off the ground but that didn't happen; maybe fertility was impossible with their immortal bodies. They stayed hidden and kept themselves out of the public eye, but that grew old.

After Opal's parents' deaths they settled into her home in St. Augustine. With Opal's interest in antiques, Alison's in literature they opened an antique store -- Relics in historical St. Augustine -- and they blended into the mystery and paranormal shroud of the city.

St. Augustine had grown, but the historic area was still cryptic and filled with the same legends of the past as if it was molded in time. Alison was never able to remove the spell on Alistair and invited him to live with them. The others were a bit unnerved by someone they couldn't see living with them, and maybe a boggart was a dangerous entity to have around. It turned out his curious nature discovered the secrets of the house. They were hidden in the walls and beneath the floorboards. This is one of the hidden journals he found.

prologue

The year 1142, I shall never forget it. 'Twas the day of my rebirth. I was seventeen and a strong, healthy young man who was quick on my feet. I shrugged my shoulders and thought, *I'm too fast, nothing will happen to me*. Like children today I never thought it would... until it did.

A raven-haired vixen with ruby lips spoke to me, pulled me from my slumber. She was like Snow White, only her intentions were anything but pure. Like a pet I ran to her, conforming to her will, against my own.

It was late August, the breeze raised the sheer white curtains from the windows, candlelight bounced off the walls. In a silken bed she lay and, like the healthy teen boy that I was, I went to her.

She seduced me. No, she forced my will. Any part of me that wanted to fight her was handcuffed metaphorically.

One bite from her succulent ruby lips subdued me and the next drained me. She offered my flail blood-let body a chalice of thick red liquid. A potion to make me the first. I craved the metallic red fuel that gives my veins life -- blood.

This night I accept my orders from our Crimson Queen. I've been chosen to accompany the night witches into the village.

Whispers through the darkness and quiet, knowing glances, tell us something is afoot. An event that will change the status of power.

For centuries we have ruled with no consequence. The humans causing havoc and pillaging more villages than us, all in the name of religion, but that may come to an abrupt end. The powers are shifting. I feel it, she feels it.

She has gifted us with compulsion, telepathy, immortality, and extreme speed. But with any gift comes a curse. We can't survive in the daylight, and remember little of our lives before the thirst.

I say this only to myself, but our job is one of the lowest standards. She gave us all these precious gifts but the worst part of our curse is we fuel her. The blood we drink drives her immortality. Anything that powers her powers us and gives us life. Therefore, we are at her mercy.

We have no will of our own. Through the blood that fuels us she speaks into our minds. No matter the distance, we can't run from her.

I am a Bloodseeker. We are Bloodseekers. Our thirst fuels the pyramid that gives what she created life.

chapter 1

"She said you were young but you are a mere child," chided the night witch. His long, dark mop tied back in a ponytail.

You will feast on my call, not before, I brain messaged my disciples waiting in the woods surrounding the village. Disdain seeping from the night witch's eyes. I wanted them to feast on him but I knew the rules.

Without responding to his snide remark I replied, "Shall we go? Time is of the essence."

He pulled his horse around. "I didn't bring an extra."

"I prefer to walk." My legs could carry me quicker than a horse. It was one of my gifts. The night witches saw me as any other Bloodseeker, not for what I truly was.

The torches' light grew brighter as we headed down the mountain. Leaving the horses tied to trees outside the village we walked in from various directions. Finding the tavern, I pushed the door wide, letting myself in.

The humans inside becoming throbbing veins and arteries calling for me. I also had the gift of self-control -- something my disciples weren't born with. It was a skill. I felt their restlessness outside the village as they also smelled the feast inside the walls.

I sipped my beer, setting the mug on the clumsy table as it unsteadily shifted beneath the force. My ears listening to the conversations, none causing any alarm. Mere humans who called themselves Christians, yet filled their nights with debauchery. In my opinion we did them a favor.

A sweet scent drifted through the smelly, unbathed men, causing me to search the room for its source. In the corner, under a hooded cloak that did little to hide her femininity. Chestnut locks crossed her porcelain cheeks. Her green eyes met mine, and for a second our gazes locked until she glanced away. No doubt I'd made her afraid.

She didn't belong here. It wasn't a place for a young woman

of her stature. Her mind became my playground as I gently eased my way into her thoughts, curious why she was in such a place. Finding her mind a tough place to impose my own, I lifted my mug and joined her.

Green eyes filled with fear widened as I drew closer. Her hand lowered to her waist as if grabbing for a knife. I chuckled inwardly. As if a mere blade could harm me. But I admired her instinct, her moxie.

Reaching her table, I pulled out the chair opposite her. "I can't help but ask why such a beautiful young maiden is hiding in a tavern," I said in a low tone barely above a whisper.

Her lips pinched as if expelling any words would bring her discomfort. She then cleared her throat and in a deep, low voice attempting to hide that she was a female replied, "You know not what of you speak."

The sweet scent poured from her lips, it was no doubt her. "Whatever you are hiding from I can help you." *Yes, I could give her something else, a place as one of my disciples.*

"There is nothing you can do for me except walk away and forget you met me." She didn't attempt to hide her voice. The tavern door swung shut and she stood, drawing her hood further over her face. "I must go now."

I glanced towards the door -- soldiers. They were no match for my skill set. I was curious, why was she hiding from them? Surely a young maiden of her stature wasn't on their wanted list. I stood. Cocking my head to catch her glance I whispered, "Stay behind me." I wasn't of formidable size but large enough to hide her small frame.

A scowl formed on her face as she relented and stayed behind me as we strode towards the door. The soldiers broke up, their eyes searching the tavern, obviously looking for someone. The chatter among the debauchers, who were moments earlier drinking and merry, suddenly changed to silence. Every floorboard creaked beneath our boots. Maybe leaving wasn't prudent, nonetheless, we were already on our way out and so continued our journey towards the door.

A staunch soldier, his shoulders broader than an ox's yoke, side-stepped in front of me, blocking the way. He pushed his hand against my chest. "Where do you think you're going?"

"The day was long and so it is time for rest," I replied in a soothing voice.

He glanced over my shoulder and pulled his sword then stepped beside me and pushed it against my back as if shoving me forward so he could glance the young maiden. "And who is this?" He brought the sword along her hood and eased it down but I caught his hand, twisted it until he dropped the sword then grabbed it in that moment, quicker than his human eyes could see, and thrust it into his chin.

All eyes were now on us. The residents sat breathless and ready to rumble. The soldiers drew their swords. I was hoping to avoid all this but wasn't left with a choice. The sword's point holding the chin of the soldier, I stated in careful words, my eyes drilling into their minds, "You will let us leave and not follow. You will continue your drinking and not remember any of this."

The soldiers put their swords away, the crowd continued their conversations and we slipped out the door.

"How did you do that?" she asked as I rushed her outside the village gates.

We slowed our pace. "It's a secret I will share with you, but not until you tell me why you are here?"

"I don't think that's any of your concern," she snapped.

"It is when someone saves your life."

"Thank you. I am grateful, but I must go." She pulled her cloak tight to fend off the night chill.

"No, it's not safe. You are staying with me."

Now, the village is yours, I mind messaged my disciples.

She huffed, "You aren't safe with me. They will come for you. Now I must go." She turned on her heel and halted when my disciples ran towards us, heading for the village gates. Their eyes heat seekers and they wouldn't spare her except I shielded her, wrapping my cloak around her.

Her body close to mine shuddered as they rushed past us, inside the walls, screams filling our ears as I slipped her over my shoulder and carried her away.

Her fear quickly subsided at her captivity. Her tiny palms pummeling my back and her own screams for me to release her louder than the dying villagers'.

chapter 2

The Crimson Queen's words echoed in my mind as I carried the maiden up the mountain. Her breathing and heartbeat returning to normal, she stopped battling me. Her strength no match to mine. *You will know by the scent of their blood if they can be reborn or used as food.* It wasn't that simple, I'd learned. The ones who fought rebirth were bull-headed, they lacked the ability to discipline themselves, attempted to refuse orders, and often went rogue, but they had their place and so I didn't destroy them.

Those who were willing embraced their fate and were the disciples I kept the closest but they, like me, had made their own rogue creatures. I needed her to want, welcome, and desire to be reborn. I set her body against the cave wall. The hood of her cloak dropped, uncovering her face. She was beautiful, more so than I imagined hidden under her cloak. Soft porcelain skin encircled by chestnut curls that poured over her shoulders.

She folded her arms defiantly over her chest, her eyes focused on the wall behind me. Unlike my disciples I didn't only see heat but retained my human vision too. I wasn't sure the Crimson Queen was aware. There were other quirks about me that set me apart from them. I kept those to myself. It was the only advantage I had. "Now, why are you running?"

She continued her stare at the wall, her lips pursed tight. I had patience but not time. "OK, I'm Alarico but you may call me Lars."

"Caty."

It wasn't much, but it was a response. "You've traveled, been to other villages. What are they saying?"

"I don't know. I keep to myself."

"Yes, and that's how you know what's being muttered."

She dropped her arms to her sides, letting her palms fall against the cave floor. "The same ole stuff," she shrugged.

Under most other circumstances I'd believe her,

except I heard a hint of deception in her tone. Before I could speak again, she said, "Why do you ask? Why do you care? You obviously don't belong to a village but are a nomad with your own agenda."

She was feisty. I changed the subject. "The soldiers were after you." I paused. "I kept you safe--"

She interrupted, "You have powers. You're a witch."

I chuckled. "No, I'm not a witch but I will share my secret after you share yours."

"You think me funny?" She raised her brows and took a deep breath. "I'm to marry an older man that I don't love. My father is... he's important and therefore so am I. Those soldiers weren't sent to kill me but retrieve me. Bring me back to a life sentence worse than death."

Nobility married nobility whether the match was wanted or not. Women didn't have the choice; their place was to obey men. "And is there a young man who you do love?"

She dropped her head. "No, but I want to make that decision and have the chance to find that love."

An idealistic young woman. If I had the capacity to love it was slowly falling for this insubordinate young lady with her devilishly delicious green eyes. I understood the lack of free will. My fate was sealed just as hers, only I couldn't run away from mine. "I'm sorry."

Her eyes softened, her fingers drawing circles in the dirt. "Have you been in love?"

"No. Now what have you heard in the villages?"

"What do you mean?"

As a human, she wouldn't be able to spot a light witch if it met her in an alley or served her a mug at a tavern, but it was worth a try. "Something quiet, something people speak of in private."

"How would I know? I've been living in alleys, hiding in barns," she snipped, taking the defensive again.

I reached into her mind again, this time not so gently. She scrunched her face and pressed her hands against her temples. "Get out of my head!"

She ejected me from her mind. Humans didn't do that. They were weak willed.

"I'll tell you!" she said, as if unaware she'd pushed me. "Just don't do that again."

"I spent the night sleeping under a hay bale in a barn, several people came, entered, unaware I was there and spoke. They talked about magic. They were witches! You see why I didn't want to tell you. Witches, and I didn't turn them in. Instead I snuck out in the morning before dawn."

"And what did these witches say?"

"They spoke in riddles about spelled stones and where the land met the sky in shades of pink and gold. I don't know what it meant and, like I said, I left before the sun came up." Her heartbeat kicked up a couple notches while she told the story. Her pulse raced beneath her skin.

"In your travels, did you see such a place?"

She nodded. "It's your turn."

I held up my hand for her to be quiet and mouthed, "There's someone outside."

I felt it more than I heard it. A rogue. Without complaint or defiance, she didn't move a muscle. I pulled my sword and walked towards the darkness leading further into the cave. Using my ears to see, a form, squat on all fours, humanoid, was lurking in a corner. "Stand, show yourself."

It scampered further into the tunnel. Smarter than it, I grabbed the girl. "We must leave here. It isn't safe for you. I'm quicker. Let me carry you."

She didn't argue, as if now realizing I saved her not only from the soldiers but the monsters -- my disciples. Fear flashed in her eyes and her voice carried into my head: *Like those you cloaked me from.* But I wasn't sure the words came from her mind or if I imagined it. Sweeping her into my arms, I ran from the cave.

Serval rogues surrounded the exit. *Her blood smells delicious. You owe us a meal.*

I owe you nothing. I would have killed you if it wasn't for our Queen. You let us go now or you will die by my sword, your black hearts pulled beating from your bodies, spilling your thick, black blood as they turn to ash.

I placed her onto her feet and pushed her behind me. "Stay close, hold onto me." Her tiny body grabbed around my middle, her fingers enclosed around my chest. She understood the fear was real, her pulse racing again. I fought my own urges to taste her blood. Her type was erotic and satiating. That is what made them so desirable to rebirth. Their blood was equivalent to an orgasm.

Stifling my urges, I drew my sword. Taking deliberate steps, I walked past the rogues who moved out of our way. Their black eyes filled with desire, their claws extended and fangs bared, noses sniffing her honey blood. I felt their breath warm on my neck as they closed in.

My speed beyond theirs, I grabbed the closest one and sliced the blade of my sword across his neck. His head hit the ground with a thump, followed by his body, and rolled as I pulled his beating black heart from his chest. They stepped backwards out of my grasp. I squished his head between my fingers. Black blood dripped from my hand, puddling in the dirt.

I held the heart up in my hands until we were clear of them, then tossed it between the group and swept Caty into my arms as we disappeared into the night.

chapter 3

"You need sleep and, by the sound of it, food." She blushed. "I'm sorry. We can keep going."

"No, we stop. They won't follow us here." I was reasonably sure they wouldn't since we were deep in light witch territory. No Bloodseeker wanted to melt from a light ball, including me, but I had something they didn't.

She nodded. "Should I gather some wood?"

I hadn't thought about that. Yes, she was probably cold. Twigs and small branches lay on the ground surrounding us. I nodded and together we collected enough wood to start a fire.

Using my heat seeking vision I searched for a meal for her. Whereas most Bloodseekers only saw through heat as the perfect hunting machine, I gained the sight but kept my own.

A few steps from us, curled on a tree, was a bird, asleep for the night, but cooked bird would quiet her complaining stomach enough for her to rebuild her strength and get a good night's sleep.

With my inhuman quickness I fetched the bird and cracked its neck.

She gasped and covered her mouth. Within moments I had it defeathered, skinned, and cooking on a long stick over the fire.

When the small morsel was cooked through, I handed her the stick.

She took it with a look of disdain but no complaints. After a couple bites she glanced at me and handed me the bird on a stick. "I'm selfish, you need food too."

Truth was I didn't. I needed human blood but, to appease her, I tore a piece off and pretended to eat, tossing it behind me when she glanced away.

She needed a proper place to sleep. Leaves would be the softest. Piling them into a small rectangle large enough for her, I stood proud. "For you."

Her a quizzical glance. I elaborated, "A place to sleep,"

She pointed to an end. "Why don't you rest here?" she said, pointing to the ground.

I didn't require it but followed her direction. The ground firm against my buttocks, she laid her head in my lap and spoke. The spillage of words from the curious female mind that I didn't look forward too.

"What were those things by the cave?"

I considered my words carefully. Was she worth the discussion? Should I tell her the truth? "They are dangerous."

"Why?"

"Their only purpose is to kill you by exsanguination"

"Are you like them?"

"No." I immediately defended myself, but I was something worse.

A Bloodseeker that could walk among the living and the rebirthed but I was no rogue.

"You are not a witch, you are not like them. What are you?"

Her hair was like silk in my hands as I let the strands move between my fingers. She was so inquisitive. I wanted to sink my teeth into her artery and taste her sweet blood. Fighting that urge I was suddenly uncomfortable. "Shh… did you hear that? " I whispered. I heard nothing but decided this was a good time to change the subject.

She nodded, her head rolling on my lap.

I whispered, "Stay here. I will check." Carefully lifting her head from my lap, I laid it gently on the leaves, bunched more just for her head and stood. Walking out into the woods, I pretended to check for the invisible noise.

This maiden had me. I didn't even think rebirthing her was an option now. No, I wanted to keep her safe.

I paced for several minutes before I faced her again. Sleeping soundly, she was.

The sun broke through the trees, giving enough shade it caused me no harm. I had spent the night watching her sleep and running my hands through her hair, letting the locks slide through and miraculously fall back into place.

She rose, her green eyes meeting mine. "Good morning."

"It is." Besides admiring her, I considered what I should do with her. Keeping her with me wasn't an option. She'd surely get devoured unless... I rebirthed her. That I didn't think was prudent. She was special but there was a place, not far where she would be safe.

chapter 4

It was on the edge of the light witch woods. We could get there by nightfall, earlier, but I needed a certain amount of shade so we'd have to stay under the cover of the trees. Full sun wouldn't kill me but it would weaken me to a useless mess.

We came upon the house of my family on the edge of the light witch woods.

"Lars." My great great niece hugged me. They knew what I was. My family had known for centuries yet never for sought me. They moved to the edge of the woods after my abduction from the Crimson Queen, seeking refuge.

"Shira." I accepted her greeting.

"And who have you brought?"

"Someone who needs a safe place. I could think of none safer than here."

She rushed us inside. "Of course. Have you been followed?" she asked, her eyes searching the woods.

"No, we traveled through the woods."

After introductions, my niece fixed Caty a meal. I took my nephew aside. "I must leave, you know that, but this girl is special. I cannot break into her mind and she sees my disciples and the rogues for what they are. Only another with special abilities can do so."

"A witch?"

"No, something else. I will return, but I must face my Crimson Queen before she questions my disappearance."

He nodded confirmation and took my hand in his. "Be careful, Lars. I don't have to tell you that, but the tension between the light and night witches is heightening. Something big is happening, something they keep under wraps. I've been able to find out little through their dreams, except the light witches have a way to destroy Bloodseekers. That will include you."

This I knew, but his confirmation made it more real. I was ready to accept my fate if it meant humans would be safe, if Caty would be safe. "You will let me know if you learn more."

"Yes, but you must sleep."

Sleep was the time I could visit others, but I couldn't control what I saw. A dream was the mind's way of sorting and sifting through what it couldn't consciously and many interesting tidbits could be found. As a Bloodseeker, my strength was weakened and I couldn't force a dream. I could merely watch and observe.

In the kitchen, Caty was helping my niece in making bread. She glanced my way, her eyes meeting mine then shifting away. I took her floured hands, grasping them in mine. She shuddered at my cold touch against her warm one but tried not to let it show. I repulsed her. Why would I think anything else? Any other thoughts I had for her needed to cease. We couldn't happen. "If you stay here you will be safe from those who seek you. This home isn't on a map or easy to find, only one with sight can stumble upon it. I will return."

Her green eyes searched mine. She nodded, pulled her hands from my grasp and folded her arms around me. "Thank you, Lars, whoever or whatever you are."

Before I returned to my queen's castle I went back to the village. My heat vision told me not a living soul existed within the walls. People lay dead against the sturdy brick walls and in the streets. Their heads tilted awkwardly. Their bodies devoid of blood. A sure sign of bloodseeker havoc. My disciples feasted and now there was but another village lost to the black death.

The galloping of horses' hooves neared the walls. Turning in the direction, I watched as the horse and rider crested the hill on a path leading into the village. I didn't hide as the horse and rider galloped towards me. The rider, a man with broad shoulders and shifty eyes, stopped within 20 feet of me.

Holding the reins, he steadied his horse. "You did this," he seethed, eyeing the dead bodies.

"The blood of these bodies isn't spilled in the streets, they are victims of the plague. The black death." He came off strong as if he was somebody but a trip through his mind told me his intentions were not those of lost family or sorrow for the villagers that lost their lives.

"So, I see, and what is the reason you visit?"

"I am traveling and was hoping for a good meal and a rest but think it is best we leave before the plague takes us."

"I have family here. I must see to a proper burial," he lied.

"Then you must. I offer you my help."

His face hardened, deep wrinkles made grooves around his eyes. "You are but a boy. Leave, I must see to this and mourn on my own."

And so it was. I stepped past him, leaving a wide berth, and when I reached the outside of the village took refuge beneath a tree and waited. He had no family and felt lucky to have arrived in time to pillage before the word got out that the village had fallen to the plague. I used my ears and heat vision to follow his movements and when he'd taken his fill of gold and silver, I waited more. Allowing him to think he was getting away with stealing from the dead.

Who was a person who could do such a thing, surely not one worth living? I thought as I slung him off his horse. It neighed and rode off into the distance. The man squirmed in my hands.

"Let me go!" he shouted and begged.

I sank my fangs into his neck and gulped as his thick red blood drained into my throat. He never saw my face as I pulled every last drop from him and tossed him into the road like the garbage he was.

Her castle built of stone, its pillars and arches high and intimidating. I pushed the heavy door, her voice reaching into my mind before I stepped a foot over the door's threshold. 'Come, Lars.'

I had no choice but to follow steps downhill into the subbasement. The upper levels home to the night witches.

Burning torches set inside sconces lit my way down the winding stone steps.

"Dear Lars." My Crimson Queen slithered off her bed. Her hair caressing my face as it pulled me towards her. Wrapping her hands around my head, she was

45

searching my mind through our blood connection. It was stronger through touch. I tucked Caty into the hidden corner of my mind. A place I was able to keep from her. The same place I was able to visit dreams. She didn't know I kept part of what I was, but I didn't think she chose me because I was a simple human but something more, something at 17 I was merely beginning to learn. It was how she captured me.

Now I was able to hide it from her, but the rest of my mind and body was hers and bent to her will against my own. The fresh blood of the thief helped mask my misdoings as his memories washed through my mind, into hers where she had to sort through them.

"My Queen, I have learned something is afoot that will kill Bloodseekers, weaken your regime. It is of the light witches in the mountains where the pink meets gold." It was better to tell her the truth than have her pry too much into my head.

She dropped her hands, long tendrils of her hair combed my back and her black pupils rolled upwards in thought. "Where pink meets gold. But you don't know which peak."

I shook my head. "No, I will find out, my Queen."

She sat on her bed, her hair tendrils dropping to the floor. "The sunrise. They are choosing a time when we must hide, but inside the mountain the darkness will hide us. We must know which one."

"I will find it," I vowed, bowing to her.

Her black eyes shifted, I felt them piercing into my soul like daggers. "You killed a rogue. Why? The girl?"

"She was of the right blood for rebirth. The rogues were in my way."

"Where is she?"

"She got away, ran into the light witch woods. I lost her there under their protection." My queen was bold but knew sending a Bloodseeker or night witch into those woods would be death.

"You were clumsy and defied my rule. Rogues have a purpose. It is not for you to make such decisions. I'm withholding my punishment for now. When it is time, I will pass down the consequences."

"Leave me," she demanded, dismissing me with a wave. "Send Marcus." Her favorite and most trusted night witch.

chapter 5

After five grueling days with Marcus, the Queen's right hand night witch, I stole a break and returned to Caty and my family. To keep my family's home safe from the Bloodseekers, I stole again through the light witch woods. Taking the chance of a radiation blast from a thousand light witches was better than my family being found.

I hadn't remembered them after my rebirth. It was they who remembered me -- my brother. He was in my clutches, his blood type right for rebirthing, but it was his words that brought me to my knees and brought back memories of my former life. *It is Mateo, your blood, your brother. We skipped stones in the river, hide and seek. Remember the time you hid in the cellar and drank our parents' aged wine? You were so drunk when I found you.* The memory rushed forward. He brought me home but I could not stay. It was then I learned that I could keep certain memories and thoughts from the Crimson Queen.

The back door of my family's home stood before me. It welcomed me even now, but I could never stay. I'd always be in the Queen's debt and mind, no matter how long I lived. The simple, stone, two story structure appeared small from the outside but inside there was plenty of room. Upstairs were four bedrooms and downstairs a kitchen, living room, and parlor for guests.

Nothing on the property appeared disturbed. The animals in the barn settled for the night, confirmed by my quick peek. Coming here was always a chance, even with the utmost caution I could bring wrath on them that would be followed with the light from a thousand light witches. I often wondered if they let me pass through the woods. Any other Bloodseeker would feel their sheer power, but I guessed it was most likely my other gift, or maybe they were watching me and waiting.

I entered, the quietness in the house agitated my anxiety. It was almost too silent as I crept up the stairs to the guest room, then the rhythmic snore of my nephew eased the anxiety. My steps were light on the wooden floors, making no noise. Caty lay on her side, golden curls covering the pillow. I lay beside her and stared at the wooden beams in the ceiling until my racing mind calmed enough that I fell into sleep.

I entered her dream. A meadow outside the fortified walls of what I imagined was her village sprawled endlessly before her. Wildflowers in bloom. Their colors vibrant as she strolled. Her hair gold in the sun's light, tied into a bun with loose curls along her cheeks. She wore a pale green gown so tight around her tiny bodice it looked uncomfortable yet showed enough cleavage to make my eyes dart to it and my mind desire her.

A maze of tall bushes materialized and, with some speculation, she entered. The sun vanished under dark clouds as she turned the first corner. A breeze caught her curls, covering her eyes. She pushed them away, continuing her journey, bend after bend she became more lost. Then a man appeared. His dark tunic and jacket displayed he was of royalty. "Demon," he hollered.

She caught her breath, eyes widened as she clutched the sides of her gown, lifting it upwards, and ran from him. Tears streamed across her cheeks, blinding her eyes. She tripped and fell into a rogue, blood running from his opened mouth as he lunged his head towards her.

"No, no," I screamed. My words went unheard, as I was only an onlooker. His mouth against her skin, she fell from him, landing in my outstretched arms. Her face a mess of tears with golden locks stuck in their wetness. "Lars?"

I awoke and curled to the side, wrapping an arm around her. I whispered in her ear, "Never will that happen to you. I won't let it." I kissed her fair, soft cheek. Her sweet blood no longer a desire for me to eat or rebirth. The pumping of her heart, its course through her vessels, meant life for her. A real life not under the Queen's control. It was then I had misgivings about being there. I put her in danger. I stole off her bed and into the night.

The woods silent as I skirted them, taking one last glance behind me, I stepped out and continued my journey back to the Queen's castle. I hadn't gone far when I heard a rustle that sounded human and smelled the sweet scent of her blood. *Why had she followed me? Had I woken her?*

It wasn't only her I smelled in the air, but Bloodseekers. Their odors becoming stronger. They were not my disciples, but rogues. I followed all the smells not far outside the light witch woods. A circle of about twenty surrounded Caty. Her heartbeat and breathing quickened in fear. She stood, her eyes darting from one to the next as she scanned the group.

Rubio, one of the first I turned, rushed her, his jagged teeth ready to dig into her skin and drain every drop of blood. I felt his desire pulse through his blackened vessels. In haste I sprinted forward, my goal to push Rubio out of the way, diverting her certain death, and slay each one. I didn't care how many I had to kill to keep her safe or how much I'd upset the Queen. Rogues had no purpose.

My steps matching Rubio's, I thrust my body into him. The force pushed him to the ground. The synchronous steps of the rogues moved backwards and they cowered. In the middle of them, Caty stood, metallic wings on her back with a razor's edge, they'd cut through her gown which dropped over her shoulders revealing the satiny tops of her breasts.

My eyes widened as I pulled myself off the ground. Rubio

crawled backwards like a spider, joining the other rogues.

I walked around her, taking in the beauty of what I saw. The wings' edges shimmered in the night and one touch cut through my finger. The rogues moved out and away, their steps quick and swift. "What are you?" I asked.

Through sniffles, she dropped her head into her hands, "I'm wrong."

"No, you are everything right," I assured her, taking her hands and lowering myself to glance into her eyes.

"You see. You see why I had to run. What's wrong with me?" she babbled.

"Nothing, nothing."

She lifted her head and wiped her tears. Her eyes carried a look of devastation.

My cut finger hadn't yet healed all the way, black blood dribbled over it. I held it out to her. "Am I wrong too?"

She touched the blood. "It's black. How?"

"We have many questions to ask each other, but am I wrong?"

She shook her head. "No, never. You have saved my life three times now."

Remembering her dream, I took her hand. "You are not a demon, but you are something more than human -- like me."

Her wings lowered on their own and flattened against her back. I took off my cape and covered her shoulders with it to hide her bare chest as we walked towards the woods. "Have you always had those?" I asked.

"No. I was born with bumps, hard bumps, on my back, spaced in equal distance from my spine -- that was all. At fifteen, they appeared for the first time and it was easy then to keep them hidden, but I knew that wouldn't last. One day I'd have to marry, then I'd be outcast, called a demon or a witch and burned like they do to the others." Her voice dropped off.

She was right. Humans wouldn't understand anything that didn't fit into the parameters their religion set. She'd be burned, and probably her family too for hiding a witch. The church would clean house. Leaving, hiding, were her only choices.

Inside the relative safety of the light witch woods we sat on a log and I told her my story. Her eyes searching mine the entire time.

"You were changed, cursed by a witch. Am I?"

"I don't think so. There are things, people out there that are something more but aren't like me – cursed -- but born that way. I don't know why, but my family is the same way -- born with special abilities that I never really developed because I was stolen and cursed before I could."

She dropped her shoulders. "You and I, people like us, will never live a normal life."

I could not deny that, but hers had more chance of being fruitful than mine. She wasn't at the mercy of the Queen but maybe something that was born to save humanity from the Queen. *Was it possible for people to be born with deformities to combat her control?* I thought so. The stories of my family and our skills only went back a couple generations before me, but the skills they now had were far more powerful than what I was born with even had I developed them further.

A female voice broke through our conversation. "Why are you here? We should kill you both."

I didn't get caught off guard much, and always expected one day a light witch would be my undoing, but I didn't think it would happen tonight. A light ball rested in her hand, illuminating a small ovular face with olive-colored skin. Out of the woods surrounding us in a

crescent moon-shape came more,
light intensifying in their palms,
threatening to melt me and
blinding my sensitive eyes so I
couldn't make out how many.

chapter 6

The one who spoke moved closer, extinguishing her light ball by simply closing her palm. The others followed. "Bloodseeker," she said, addressing me. "The only reason you are still alive is that we have seen you, watched you in these woods many times. You always visit the house on the edge. The family that sought our protection many generations ago. You don't bring them harm, so we let you pass, but our eyes are on you at all times. We know your thoughts and intentions."

She paced. "Many times, you've considered whether we knew you were here and wondered why we never killed you. Now you bring us a maiden, one with a unique gift. It scared the Bloodseekers as they thought she was one of us, but she is something else.

"Why should we offer either of you protection?"

I responded, "You don't need to offer me protection. I only come through the woods so others of the night won't find my family, but you know that and let me pass. She is the one who needs protection." I glanced at Caty. "They were scared tonight but their thirst will outweigh that in the end. She is something special, maybe something that can help you with your war on the Bloodseekers."

"Both of you, come with me," she said in haste. Turning on her heel she led us, followed by the team of other light witches, deep into the woods.

Stopping within sight of a small cabin, she turned and met both our gazes. "Abriel has the wisdom of many generations. She not only hears your thoughts and feels your emotions but sees the future. She will know what to do with the girl."

"Thank you," I said.

She didn't respond in words but continued up the path to the cabin and knocked on the door. A small maiden, who didn't appear more than thirteen, opened the door. She was ordinary in appearance, thin, wisps of hair hung over her shoulders, straight lips set inside her heart-shaped face. She opened the door wide, letting us in.

A fire roared inside the stove and furnishings were sparse. My eyes looked past the drabness of the small, humble home and went to a painting on the wall. Then forgot the out of place painting when Abriel padded towards Caty. She took her hands. Abriel's head dropped backwards, her body very still for a few long, breathless moments. I had never been this close to a light witch and knew little about their magic except the light balls they produced in their palms. That was all I needed to know since it was the thing that could kill me. I didn't know if a single witch could cause my death but I never wanted to find out either.

Abriel lifted her head and, glancing at the other witches, she seemed to send them a message as they left the cabin. "Now that we are alone. Yes, Caty, you are important. There are things that will happen but it is not what the other witches may think. You will not save humanity, instead you will give rise to others who will one day defeat the Sorceress." Her eyes bore into mine. They called my Queen 'the Sorceress' as that's what she'd been before she created us, becoming one of us first.

"You, Alarico, need to live. Your life is one of value but we cannot protect you or help you. Not for three nights or ever. You will leave the girl with me. She will be safe."

As much as I couldn't bear to leave Caty, Abriel was right. She couldn't stay with me. "I must ask, even though you will deny me an answer. The light witches are planning our demise even now. If my life has value, please allow me to help you. I will work both sides."

She moved, stepping in front of a painting. "You are correct. I can't reveal anything." She turned, facing the painting. "Your place is at the Sorceress' side. Her trust in you is what makes your life valuable. One day, all this will make sense and you will remember my words. Now you must leave us." She gently pressed a finger on the painting.

It was Majorca, an island in the Balearic Sea. It was oddly out of place in her cabin and an item that my eyes went to right away. Now she brought deliberate attention to it.

"Have you ever visited?" she asked, lowering her hand and turning towards us.

"No," Caty and I both responded.

"You should. It is quite picturesque." She waved me off in dismissal. *Don't return Bloodseeker*, her words spoke directly into my mind. Their connotation, the inflection of her mind words, were devoid of threat.

I turned to Caty, placing my hands on her shoulders. I couldn't say goodbye. It didn't feel right. Instead I kissed the top of her head and left.

Abriel's words played through my head. She expected me to come back. 'Not for three nights' were her words. It didn't make sense in any other context than a clue. The fourth day, during sunrise when the pink meets the gold.

The sandy beaches and high peaks in the picture stayed on my mind. Majorca, that was it. Where the pinks met the golds. It would be sunrise or sunset. She knew I would understand, but why did she tell me? Was all this merely a game between the light witches, something to throw off the Bloodseekers? The Sorceress as they called her?

Marcus and I were wrong, thinking it was Pena de Moratalla. *Why would she show me the correct one?* This had to be a trick. Maybe Moratalla was it and she was deflecting us. If she reached into my mind, she'd know I'd rather lead the Queen away from the truth. My mind was conflicted on the slow walk home. My pace hampered by doing what was safest for Caty, running in circles around Abriel's words.

The chatter of humans sounded in my ears, rushing silently through the woods, a group of soldiers had camped out for the night. They were rising, their horses still tethered to trees. Their hearts thumped inside my head. Their lives meant nothing, as little was worse than anyone associated with the church. That alone was a vile act. I went straight for the one who appeared to be in charge, sinking my teeth into his neck, gulping his blood that pumped freely into my mouth and down my chin.

The other ran away like bugs but they couldn't hide from me out of the woods. My heat vision found them. The sun burned against my skin, parching it like paper. I welcomed the pain as one by one I sucked them dry. Blood was spilled over the ground and down their necks. Licking them clean, I left them together -- victims of the black death. The plague that knew no end, nor did it care about religion and the practices of the church.

chapter 7

My Crimson Queen stared at me, her eyes searching mine, her mind inside my own. There was never any other answer than to tell her the truth, so why I'd fretted so much, I didn't know. The Queen would make up her own mind. "Where were you and why do you smell of light witch?" She turned her nose upwards as if disgusted.

"I went out to find a human to eat but was taken by a group of light witches. They took me into their woods and grilled me under their lights." She glanced at my skin that wasn't yet all the way healed.

"They wanted to know why Marcus and I were searching Pena de Moratalla. It was a young one who let Majorca slip. I caught the word in her mind."

She stepped back. "They are trying to trick us. She didn't let anything slip. In your weakened state she let you into her mind. It is not Majorca, but either way we will be waiting."

"There is one more thing, my Queen," I said, waiting for her response.

"What is that?"

"It will happen the morning after three nights. Let me take my disciples and we will wait inside the mountain for them. They will not get past us."

A sinful smile played on her lips. "This isn't a job for your disciples. They will be coming with us to the new world when this is finished. It is a job for the rogues. I have told you they have a purpose and this is it. Nothing in my kingdom is expendable until I say so and your punishment for killing a rogue is to gather them and command them into the mountain. If any survive, I will give them their freedom."

I didn't dare ask about the new world. I had heard nothing of this until now, but I wasn't privy to her wishes unless they concerned me. "Very well."

"Clean yourself, you look disgusting," she demanded as I exited her quarters.

There was only one thing the rogues wanted more than their freedom and that was blood --

Caty's blood. I felt them always as the one who rebirthed them. I, like the Queen, always felt them. I could hear their thoughts when tuned in. I turned my mind to them, listening in when the plan came to me.

When nightfall came, I sought out the rogues as they devoured the innocent residents of a farmhouse, taking the men, women, and children. They hadn't noticed me as I waited at the edge of the property. Once finished with their feast, Rubio, one of my first rebirthed, spotted me. I'd often wondered why they didn't get caught and killed. Their lack of sense and self, absent during their feeding. Many had been died at the hands of light witches, but not enough.

"We didn't leave any for you," he seethed as he stepped closer. "That's right, you only eat those you find morally wrong. Isn't that what you tried to teach us." His mocking was obvious.

"I have something to offer you," I jested.

"We're listening," other rogues gathered.

"The Crimson Queen will give you your freedom in exchange for something."

Rubio's lack of surprise was most likely due to his disbelief that the Queen would give them anything, especially freedom. "What is the exchange?"

"The light witches are planning something. We know where and when. Your job is to stop them."

I probed into his mind as he considered my words. It seemed too easy, yet they knew the threat of a light witch meant certain death, but if they weren't expected, and had the element of surprise, then killing a group of light witches and feasting on their blood wasn't impossible. It wasn't enough though.

"That is suicide. Our freedom will mean nothing if we are dead. We need something more." His stance shifted as he rocked on his feet and wrapped his arms across his chest.

I had almost counted on that. "I will give you the maiden. Drink her, rebirth her. She will be yours if you live."

"The winged girl. Why would we want to drink her?"

"Because she is something more than human. I feel your desire to taste her. It dominates you," I responded. My plan wasn't to get her killed, but the opposite. She would live, they would die. Light witches did nothing without light.

"And what of the night witches, will they not offer us protection?" Rubio said in an attempt to bargain.

"I have given you the offer. Either take it or don't," I said, turning on my heel and walking away.

"Stop," Rubio shouted. "We accept the offer."

Like the poor excuse for a being of any kind that they were, they couldn't resist the two things they wanted even if it meant their lives in exchange.

chapter 8

With the rogues in place at both sites, I returned to Abriel. She opened the door, her straight lips curled into a smile. Allowing me inside the cabin she said, "You're as clever as I thought. Much smarter than the other bloodseeking, mindless monsters. She awaits you."

"You know?" I asked.

"We have eyes and ears everywhere, especially on you. We had to know you would make the best decision and you have."

Caty stepped out of a room, a red cloak around her shoulders. She was a vision, an angel if there was ever one. "I'm ready, Lars."

I couldn't mess this up. It had to play out the way it had in my mind many times over the past couple days. If I wasn't a Bloodseeker my palms would be sweaty with nerves. She rode on a horse as I walked alongside, my stride keeping pace. The ride was a silent one. What the witch showed her I could only imagine but thought maybe it was nothing as our actions had to play out as her vision. Any disruption to that could change events, or so I thought.

We reached the Pena de Moratalla. The rogues inside the mountains, stationed in the tunnels waiting in silence to kill the witches. Even in the distance between us and Majorca I heard the rogues' screams as my skeleton crew sent there was burned with light and sliced with swords. That was the Queen's wrong in giving this to me as a punishment. Caty heard nothing as she stepped off the horse, ready to face her fate.

I would keep her safe for as long as possible but was ready to meet my death along with all the rogues. Their movement inside the tunnels of the mountain moved closer. They too had heard the cries of the rogues. We were all bound by blood. The rush of them poured from the mouth of the mountain.

"You deceived us!" Rubio screamed as he charged towards me. I threw him aside but more were on me. It wasn't going the way I'd planned. Through the mass of rogues on top of me, Caty's wings spread out, followed by the rogue screams then the light covered us. It was brilliant. One by one the rogues turned to ash. When the throng of them was gone and the sun hailed its brightness on me, Caty ran to me, lowered herself and covered me with her wings.

Once the light was gone, she lifted herself upwards. She was no longer human, but something else. Her face that of a large bird with a solid beak meant for eating flesh, and a tail. Her feet and hands like claws with thick talons.

"You are the most magnificent being I've ever seen," I said, awestruck.

Within moments she was again human. Her body shifting in segments. Claws and beak returning first followed by her tail, body, and last, wings. In her nakedness she reached for my hand, assisting me to my feet.

"Did you know?" I had to ask. Maybe the witches helped her find the being within.

"I didn't know my wings would save you. It was an instinct that I should cover you."

"The other you..."

She nodded. "I didn't know that either. It was Abriel's words that helped me find it. She told me to let the energy flow into me, overtake me. In my fear, that's what I did. I didn't try to stop it but accepted it, breathed it life as I felt it overcome me."

I clutched her face, pressing my palms over her cheeks, and kissed her lips. She welcomed the intrusion and met my passion with

her own. I was very much in love
with this Caty. Her other side
excited me, aroused me. In that
moment before the sun rose over
the peak, we made love. The ashes
of the rogues surrounding us.

chapter 9

The daylight sun too bright for me, we retreated inside the mountain. "You are free now. Dead, nobody will search for you again. You can live with the witches," I said, smoothing Caty's wild curls that always bounced back into place.

Her head in my lap, she crunched her brows. "And what of you? You are dead too. The light turned you to ash like the others."

"No, my Queen senses me. I must go. If not, she will search for me, sparing no lives, all are expendable."

Her green eyes stared up at me. "How will I find you?"

"You won't ever. Don't search for me, not here or the new world. Nowhere, ever. Promise me," I demanded.

"You go to the new world, away from the witches who kill your kind."

"It's more complicated than that. Witches cover the globe. We are merely starting again in a world that doesn't know my kind. We can never run away completely, or far enough. I had accepted my death, the light from the radiation on my face. Its nip at my skin felt good as I welcomed the end of my pathetic existence." It was true. I hadn't wanted to be saved but, sitting with her now, I was pleased she'd saved me. If it was the only joyous moment I'd share for the remainder of my days, it was worth it.

She rose upward and sat up straight. "We shouldn't prolong our departure then. Evening is here," her words short, I'd hurt her feelings.

The walk home was quiet this time because neither of us wanted to say goodbye, to speak of a life without the other. I didn't enter the light witch woods, as surely they'd execute me. That was the warning in Abriel's words. In three nights. That was the only time they were going to let me pass.

I stopped as her horse trotted to the edge of the woods. She pulled the reins and the animal obeyed, staying put. She turned her head and eyed me over her shoulder. "I'm glad I met you, Lars."

My heart was about to burst. I hurried to her side. "I love you, Caty."

"It's Catherine." She smiled demurely. "I love you, Alarico, and will never forget all you did for me."

Our lips met in one last kiss before she trotted into the woods I was no longer welcome to enter.

chapter 10

I made the ship as my Crimson Queen waited on me. She knew well that I was alive. It took many nights to sail across the Atlantic, settling in a land that stayed warm all year. Its lush landscape offering shade from the forbidden sun. A few humans built a city and defended it with forts along the ocean and river. Over time, the area became more crowded and settlers called the city St. Augustine.

My Queen never asked about that day. I'd paid my price and so had the rogues. She hadn't any idea the witches' plan had come to fruition, but she would know in the next several years following that day when the first Slayers acquired their amulets, finding ways to kill Seekers. They hunted us, with gifts special to them. It was a relentless hunt as we fought to stay alive, many Bloodseekers losing their lives and very few Slayers. They regenerated their powers quickly. Only seven youths, it seemed like more. They were everywhere all the time.

It was many years later, the battle between Slayers and Bloodseekers raging, when I saw her again. I'd spent the years watching her in her dreams, but seeing her face to face all my feelings for Caty rushed to the surface, back to that day when we killed the rogues. Even in old age she was beautiful.

Her golden hair now a crown of white, her soft, taut skin filled with wrinkles. I'd never have grown old with her, even had I been able to escape my Queen. The realization hit me then, hard, when I looked into her weary green eyes.

"Alarico, it's time you knew our destiny, our purpose. After you left, I learned I was with child. We have a daughter. She is like you and like me but like neither of us. Alondra can change into the form of any living creature. She calls herself a shiftling."

From that moment I welcomed my daughter, buried her mother, and made an alliance with the light witches who'd protected them. With my help, the Slayers learned where to find the Bloodseekers, to harm them where they hurt, and the battle became lopsided as the second generation of Slayers was able to connect hands and send a light across the globe, killing every Bloodseeker on the surface.

It wasn't witches who protected me. I gave them intel in return for nothing. My pleasure was watching the Bloodseekers die and the Queen's pyramid of power struggle to stay afloat. It was sheer luck that I wasn't destroyed along with so many others. The light witches had many gifts, one of those the gift of future sight. They knew all along how the future would play out, at least the ones with sight. Like Abriel, I doubted they told all to everyone. We were all pawns in a future that had to play out. My destiny wasn't over and so I lived.

It was an unlikely alliance with Isandro, one who missed the rebirth, only being half complete, he saves others like him. Together we have saved many. They drink the blood of animals as a drop of human blood is what completely changes a human into a Bloodseeker after the bites. With him I leave this book to be found in the future when I hope I no longer live and, if there is an afterlife, will meet my Caty and Alondra.

Alarico hidden journals volume 2

Cayto

hidden journals volume 3

chapter 1

The summer after high school graduation was a pinnacle moment in time. A turning point that changed the course of my life. Careless Whisper by George Michael brings the memories back as if I was still living in that moment.

In between homes as my parents just sold our home, we spent the summer in a small town. The house, with its large, sinister peaks and round parlor and upstairs game room, was the place one expected shadows in the corners, monsters in the basement, and Hellraiser in the attic. In the tiny town of Aster, Georgia it was sorely out of place like the Addams Family surrounded by the Brady Bunch. Maybe we were the Addams Family.

I'd taken a job at the town nursery, only a couple blocks from the house. Working outside in the sweltering heat, my chest was covered in sweat. I walked behind the building and pulled my shirt off, stuffed part of it into my back pocket. The rest hung against my leg. Shaking a Marlboro from the pack, I lifted it to my mouth and flicked my finger.

A small flame balanced on the tip of my finger, which I used to light the cigarette, and took a drag.

"Got an extra?" came a voice sweet as chocolate cheesecake. A girl, her long, black hair swinging in a ponytail stepped beside me and rested her back against the wall. She wore an Aster Grill uniform. It looked like something from the TV show Flo in light pink with turned up pointed sleeves and a collar low enough to get a glimpse of cleavage but not enough to dream of nipples.

I shook out another. When she brought it to her lips I gave her mine to light it since I didn't have an actual lighter and showing her my witch powers wasn't an option.

"Thanks." She propped a foot against the wall as she took a drag. "You must be new."

"How'd you guess?" Yes, it was a sarcastic answer.

"When someone enters a town of 1,583 residents, one notices." She chuckled. "It was a stupid question. So, what are you doing here? It's not like this place is on a map."

She lifted the cigarette to her red, heart-shaped lips and ran a hand through her straight, dark bangs. They flopped back into place. Her high cheek bones, olive skin, and dark almond-shaped eyes gave away her Asian heritage. She was far too beautiful to be stuck in a town like this. I redirected my attention back to her question. "My family. I'll be in college in the fall. What about you?"

"I don't plan on making a living from the diner like Jolene and Judy. Geez, that's no future." Doing a conversation one-eighty her dark eyes brightened. "What are you doing after work?"

"Thought I'd walk down to town hall and back to get a proper tour of the town."

She giggled. "You'll have to make it past town hall to the motel. That's a proper tour. Meet me here and I'll show you around later." She flicked the cigarette, her eyes quickly traveling over my chest before they darted back to my face.

"I'm off at seven."

She wrinkled her nose. "I know," she said, pointing to an old sign resting against the wall near us with the nursery's hours of business on it. "See you then."

"What's your name?" I called as she walked away.

"Malina," she answered without looking back. "What's yours?"

"Cayto."

She paused and turned towards me. "See you at seven Cayto." Then she rushed back to the diner.

chapter 2

By 7:15 I waited by the back entrance to the nursery. I lit a Marlboro as I waited, hoping I hadn't missed her. I figured she had until my cigarette was finished before I'd accept she stood me up.

I tossed the butt to the ground and smashed the smoldering end with my shoe then pushed off the wall to head home.

"Hey there."

I glanced up and there she was. Her shiny hair let loose from its earlier ponytail. She'd changed into shorts that hugged every curve and a half shirt displaying her flat stomach. A strap from her bag crossed her chest. Great! She looked amazing and I looked like someone who'd spent the day working in a nursery.

As if she'd read my mind she said, "I always bring street clothes. I hate that uniform." She visibly shuddered.

"It's not so bad. You look like Asian Flo."

"Asian? Who says I'm Asian?"

"I... um..."

Her lips curled into a smile as I fumbled over my words, trying to find the right ones so I didn't make a huge ass of myself.

She play punched my chest. "You're so serious. My mom's side has Asian - Eskimo or something. My brother is a blue-eyed Caucasian. Weird how things mix.

Sometimes people think one of us was adopted but I look like my aunt and he looks like my dad."

"So, what do you do for fun in this too-small-for-a-map town?"

"We don't hang out here." She grabbed my hand and pulled me towards a back road behind the nursery.

I felt small compared to her. She was glorious, perfect and outgoing. I'd never been called unattractive and even been called "hot" by many girls my age with my jet black, thick waves that were now reaching past my shoulders and dark blue eyes. But I paled to her beauty. From the inside out she radiated.

We strolled through the woods. "I look like shit," I finally said.

"No, you don't. Got a little farmer's tan going on though." She touched my arm beneath my rolled sleeve.

"Yeah." Immediately, I slid the rolls down.

"Stop. You can be perfect in college. Today you're a working man on a tour of Aster, Georgia with me."

I didn't know what that meant but her hands against my arm felt good. A small tingle buzzed through me.

I pulled my shirt upwards and she moved her hands as I slid it over my chest and head then tucked it partly into my pocket.

"Well, that's even better! You have nice muscle definition."

Shy and coy were two words she didn't appear to understand the meaning of. I was already attracted to her sheer forwardness.

"Come on." She grabbed my hand again and ran like she had a purpose. At 6'2" it didn't take much to keep up with her as I scrambled through the woods to a small clearing. A large wooden chalet was at the edge.

She skirted the clearing until we were close to the house then paused and glanced down at a cellar door. It opened from the middle with a handle on each side of the doors.

I stared at the chalet. "We can't go down there, someone lives here."

"Trust the local girl. Help me out." She grabbed a handle and lifted.

I grabbed the other handle, hoping I wasn't breaking and entering.

Without hesitation she bounced down the steps with me following. She pulled a light, illuminating the space. Rows of wine lined every wall.

"This old man owns this place but he's only here in the winter and doesn't ever lock the cellar. We've been coming here for years. Never seems to notice. All the good stuff is upstairs, unless you like wine?"

"He just leaves the door unlocked?"

She wrinkled her cute Asian nose. "Something like that."

I was already in deep, so what the heck. I followed her up the stairs and into the house.

The large room before us had an open design with the kitchen and family room occupying one large space. Plush sectionals rested before a large screen TV with an entertainment system filled with movies.

"Pick out a movie while I get us drinks."

She was so casual about the whole thing. What the hey, might as well be comfortable and drunk when they loaded me into the cop-wagon.

Within a couple minutes she handed me a drink and another and another while we watched the movie.

I'd never met anyone like her and figured she was one of a kind.

She jumped off the couch. "Here's the fun part," she said as she stripped her shirt off, revealing two perfectly round breasts inside a lacy bra. Before I could react, she unzipped her pants, pulled them down and tossed them aside. Her ass and stomach were pristine. She giggled and ran towards the front door then swung it open to the night.

I didn't hesitate in unzipping my shorts, letting them drop, and following her. I was in far too deep and she was too perfect.

She staggered backwards, checking out my goods. "We run naked through the woods," she yelled as she took off, bare feet smashing over the tall grass.

I followed her sweet ass in its lacy panties into the woods. I caught up to her quick enough and she stopped abruptly. I skidded to a halt just shy of running into her.

"Doesn't it feel good?" She spun in circles then tripped, landing on her ass.

I couldn't react fast enough to catch her so I offered her laughing ass a hand and she pulled me toward her. I landed face down beside her. The strength in her grip surprised me.

Rolling to my back, I stared up at the trees obscuring most of the stars, but the crescent moon was bright.

"It's beautiful isn't it?" She paused for a moment than did another conversation one-eighty. "I hate this town. I hate it!" she said in distaste. "My parents expect me to stay here but there's nothing here. I hate it."

I raised up on my arm to stare at her pouty face. "Why?" A stupid thing to say, but it was all that came to mind.

"Some shit about duty and whatever. You're lucky you get to go to college. I'm stuck with community college."

"So, get out of here. It's your life."

"Yeah, maybe if I can save enough at my diner job." Her words dribbled in annoyance.

"It's beautiful here. I've never felt so close to the heavens."

"Yeah, there's all types of beauty." She glanced at me with her brown velvet eyes. "You want to see something else?"

I shrugged. "Sure."

She jumped up and stagger-walked to the chalet with its door wide open.

After we put our clothes back on, she locked the front door and went back through the cellar.

Crickets chirped and owls hooted as we traipsed through the woods to another undisclosed location. She was adventure in an approximate five-foot-tall, one-hundred-pound frame. I'd have followed her off a bridge if it meant being close to her.

"You live in that green house, right?"

I didn't bother to ask how she knew. In a town of 1,583 residents, it probably was easy enough to figure out.

"It has a history."

"Like what?"

"The original residents disappeared. It went to the family but they just rent it out. It's not often they find renters and when they do, they never stay long."

"I can see that. It's pretty creepy but it's only a house and we're only here for the summer."

"Maybe." She stopped as if she had more to say but reconsidered.

Long strands of straight hair had fallen across her face, obscuring its beauty. I pushed them back. The touch of her soft skin against my hand sent more electricity buzzing through me. "You're beautiful."

"So are you. Not like any guy I've ever met. You're diff-er-ent." She pronounced each syllable as she stared into my eyes, my soul. Their radiance burned through me.

My lips parted and my neck leaned as I brushed my mouth against her rose petal-soft lips. They parted, accepting my kiss. They swirled in hunger and a buzz radiated throughout my body. It was love at first kiss. No, first sight. I was immersed the moment I saw her.

Our kiss under the trees and stars was interrupted by snarling.

Our lips and tongues untangled as we both stared wide-eyed at the creatures surrounding us. They were like large wolves but looked more like bull dogs only much, much larger.

In a moment my instinct and magic kicked in. I pulled her towards me with one hand and sent a spinning fire tornado towards the dogs. It blew towards them and they lowered their heads and pawed the ground with growls of complaint and threat.

My mind so focused on protecting her, I didn't notice what she did until a light ball blasted through the air towards the furry beasts.

"What are you doing, Malina?" asked a male voice.

"Freeman, show yourself."

I was too perplexed with saving her from the beasts to notice her nonchalant voice. My heart was beating fast.

From the woods emerged a young man, our age. I glanced his way for a second then back at the beasts, but they were gone.

I twisted, searching for them. "Didn't you see..." *Was I going crazy?*

She jabbed my gut. "We did see, but they weren't real. It was my brother."

I stared at the young man. "You need to get home," he ordered her.

"We were hanging out." She stabbed the words at him.

"With a night witch!" The young man's voice grew firm and that's when I got it. He was her brother and fulfilling his light witchy brother duty of saving her from the night witch.

I never got over that weakness when I was with her. It was like my own witch went into hiding surrounded by her glory.

They were light witches. We came from two very different worlds. One that protected Earth's inhabitants from Bloodseekers or,

in common language, vampires and
the other was the Bloodseekers'
born ally -- night witches.

Alarico hidden journals volume 2